Bob's Bake Shop

by Miriam Sklar

ISBN: 978-1-338-75071-3
Illustrated by John Lund

Published by Scholastic Inc., 557 Broadway, New York, NY 10012

10 9 8 7 6 5 4 68 25 26 27/0

Printed in Jiaxing, China. First printing, January 2021.

Bob sells pies.

Bob sells cupcakes.

Bob sells bread.

Bob sells donuts.

Bob sells cookies.

Bob sells small cakes.

Bob sells tall cakes!